SCOTT COUNTY LIBRARY
SHAKOPEE, MN 55379

Mardi Gras

Michelle Lee

World's Greatest Celebrations: Mardi Gras

Copyright © 2017
Published by Scobre Educational
Written by Michelle Lee

All rights reserved.

Printed in the United States of America.

No part of this book may be reproduced in any manner whatsoever without written permission, except in the case of brief quotations embodied in critical articles and reviews.

Scobre Educational
42982 Osgood Road
Fremont, CA 94539

www.scobre.com
info@scobre.com

Scobre Educational publications may be purchased for educational, business, or sales promotional use.

Cover and Layout by Sara Radka
Edited by Lauren Dupuis-Perez
Copyedited by Malia Green
Images sourced from iStock, Shutterstock, Alamy, and Newscom

ISBN: 978-1-62920-570-0 (hardcover)
ISBN: 978-1-62920-569-4 (eBook)

Table of Contents

Introduction 4
An introduction to Mardi Gras

History 6
The Spring Festival, Lent and Carnival, the Birth of New Orleans and Mardi Gras

The Colors of Mardi Gras 12
Purple, Yellow, and Green

Location 14
New Orleans's Past and Present, the Krewe of Zulu

Meaning 16
Having Fun

Special Events 18
Parades, Costumes, and Gifts; Zulu and Rex

What Sets it Apart 20
Fans and Performers

Highlights 22
Masks and Masquerade Balls, Krewes, Throws, Hurricane Katrina

Around the World 26
Other parts of Louisiana; Mobile, Alabama; Rio de Janeiro, Brazil; Martinique

The People 28
One Million People a Year, Famous People in the Mardi Gras Parade

Impact 30
Visitors, Places, and Events

Glossary 31
Key Words and Definitions

Introduction

Mardi Gras (pronounced *mar-dee grah*) is a French **Creole** celebration in New Orleans, Louisiana. It takes place every year on the Tuesday before **Ash Wednesday**. Mardi Gras is part of a bigger celebration called Carnival, a party that has been celebrated for hundreds of years. Carnival is all about letting go of the bad things in life and having fun.

Carnival starts on January 6 and ends on the day of Mardi Gras. Carnival is four to eight weeks long, while Mardi Gras is only one day. Mardi Gras is the last day of Carnival, so it is the most colorful and happiest day of the celebration. The streets are packed with people. There are parades, **floats**, **masquerade balls**, costumes, jazz music, dancers, and clowns. The costumes are similar to the ones you see on Halloween. People wear bright, sparkling clothes and have necklaces with purple, yellow, and green beads. Some wear masks while others wear big hats with glitter and feathers.

When is Mardi Gras?

Mardi Gras is always 46 days before Easter, but since Easter's date changes every year, it can be hard to figure out which Tuesday Mardi Gras will be on. Here are some dates:

2017 – February 28
2018 – February 13
2019 – March 5
2020 – February 25

The biggest event is the street parades. They last the whole day. The floats are beautifully decorated and carry people dressed like royalty. Each float has its own king and queen who wave to the people and shower them with gifts. People yell, "Throw me something, Mister!" and the float riders throw small things like beaded necklaces, candy, cake, **doubloons**, and toys. If you visit Mardi Gras, bring big bags so you can hold all the free stuff you catch!

Brazilian dancer Karina Marcelino is all dressed up and ready to dance the samba during Carnival in Florianópolis.

History

Mardi Gras comes from a medieval festival in Europe. Hundreds of years ago, Europeans celebrated the spring season. People planted new seeds, and prayed that those seeds would grow into strong and healthy crops. Some people had parades and let a fat bull run around the village. The bull represented good health and plenty of food. The people hoped they would be healthy and have lots of good things to eat. During the spring festival, they would dance, sing, play games, and be merry. It was a time of new beginnings and great joy for the year to come.

In the ninth century, a new religion began to spread all over Europe. This was Christianity, and it changed the way Europeans celebrated spring. They began to celebrate the season of Lent. Lent is not a festival, but a time of prayer and fasting. During Lent, Christians give up parties and favorite foods, like meats or sweets, in order to become closer to God.

Because the season of Lent is a time of sacrifice, the days leading up to Lent started to focus on fun and indulgence. People began to call this time Carnival. Just like its meaning today, Carnival was a time to celebrate with family and friends, play games, eat sweets, and have fun. Over time, the last day of Carnival became the most important because it was the last day people could have fun before Lent. This is why the French named this day Mardi Gras, or "Fat Tuesday." It is the last time people can enjoy themselves and eat lots of good, fatty foods.

DID YOU KNOW?

Carnival comes from the Latin words *carne vale*, meaning "goodbye to meat."

This is an Italian celebration of Carnival in the 15th century. People are having fun and eating lots of food.

At the stroke of midnight, Mardi Gras ends and Lent begins. Some Christians begin to fast, which means not eating anything at all for a short time. They still have meals, but eat less than they usually do. Lent lasts for six weeks. After that, Christians stop fasting and celebrate with large meals and parties during Easter.

In the 19th century, people held Carnival balls with fancy costumes and dancing.

In 1699, Mardi Gras was brought to America from France. French explorers sailed to America and stopped at what is now Louisiana. When they got there, the explorers were very sad because it was the day of Mardi Gras and they knew they were missing a big celebration back at home. In honor of the day, they named the spot where they stopped "Mardi Gras Point." Soon after that, more French people travelled to Louisiana and settled there. Over time, they built the city of New Orleans.

The Krewe of Comus parade during Mardi Gras in New Orleans

In 1857, several young men formed the first Carnival club in New Orleans. They named it Comus after the Greek god of fun. During Mardi Gras, the Comus club members wore masks, fancy costumes, and brought the first floats to the city. You can still find Comus riding through the parades today.

After Comus, more clubs began to appear. These clubs are called krewes and Rex is the most important krewe of all. This is because Rex has the largest parade featuring some of the most beautiful floats and decorations. Those who are chosen as King and Queen by Rex are celebrated as the King and Queen of the whole New Orleans celebration. Rex also rides in parades with a bull just like in olden times. However, the bull is now made of paper.

The Krewe of Zulu is an African-American club with a long history in New Orleans.

Zulu is also an important krewe. It is an African American club that is named after an African tribe. Zulu has great costumes and bands in its parade. People also look forward to the things that they throw. If you're lucky, you might catch one of Zulu's famous hand-painted coconuts!

The king of the Krewe of Zulu greets watchers during the 2015 Mardi Gras parade in New Orleans.

The Colors of Mardi Gras

Purple represents justice.

12 WORLD'S GREATEST CELEBRATIONS

Gold, or yellow, represents power.

Green represents faith.

Mardi Gras 13

Location

New Orleans has a rich history that shaped the Mardi Gras we celebrate today. It is a history of new beginnings and explorations, but also a time filled with problems. In the 1800s, New Orleans was a large and wealthy city, but some Southerners still practiced slavery.

After the Civil War, African American slaves were freed, but many people were still **prejudiced** against African Americans. Mardi Gras parades were still held, but African Americans were not allowed to participate. During the 1900s, the Krewe of Rex was an all-white parade. A black man named William Storey was upset by this, and he decided to make fun of Rex. While King Rex was crowned and dressed in his fanciest costume, William put an old, greasy can on his head and wrote the words "King Zulu" on it. Then he copied the movements of King Rex and followed him for the whole parade. People thought it was funny and the tradition stuck. This is how the Krewe of Zulu came to be.

During the 1900s, African Americans were not allowed to participate in Mardi Gras parades in New Orleans.

Now King Rex and King Zulu greet each other as a reminder of equality.

Today, King Zulu is more elegant and dressed just as nicely as Rex. This parade hasn't lost its sense of humor, though. Zulu is still one of the funniest and most amusing parades. Both King Rex and King Zulu now greet each other as equals.

Did you know?

New Orleans is the birthplace of jazz, a type of music inspired by both European and African influences. It is often played during Mardi Gras.

Mardi Gras

Meaning

Mardi Gras has many meanings. To medieval Europeans, Mardi Gras was a day to celebrate spring. To Christians, it is a celebration before a time of reflection and fasting. It is also a continuation of Christmas. Another name for Mardi Gras is Carnival. Carnival begins on January 6 and lasts about four to eight weeks. Christians believe that January 6 was the day that three wise kings came to visit baby Jesus and give him gifts. Carnival is a continuation of this celebration of new life, joy, and gift-giving.

Carnival is a time for happiness and amusement.

Many people eat the colorful King Cake during Mardi Gras.

Even though this celebration has a religious history, joining in on the fun is for everyone. Just think of circuses, rides, sweets, and games. Chances are you've been to or heard about a carnival in your neighborhood before. We have these carnivals because of this holiday, which was celebrated hundreds of years ago.

Did you know?

A popular food item during Mardi Gras is King Cake. The cake is large and shaped like a doughnut. It is covered in purple, yellow, and green icing—the official colors of Mardi Gras. It is tradition to buy one and share it with friends. In every King Cake, there is a baby doll that is baked inside. But be careful. Whoever finds the doll has to hold a party for their friends, or buy the next King Cake!

Special Events

The day of Mardi Gras is the largest and most special part of the Carnival celebration. The Krewe of Zulu is the first parade to appear. They start around 8:30 in the morning, and move through downtown New Orleans. Thousands of performers are in the Zulu parade. Many wear bright, dazzling costumes with dark face paint. Some are in floats as tall as houses, while others walk on the streets. The people walking are usually dancers, jazz players, or school marching bands. The float riders call out to the audience and throw beads, flowers, and stuffed animals. Zulu is also famous for its decorated coconuts. It would hurt if someone hit you on the head with a coconut, though, so Zulu hands coconuts to people instead of throwing them. They especially like giving gifts to children rather than to adults.

After Zulu comes Rex, the biggest and fanciest parade of all. One way you can tell that Rex is there is by the large, painted bull that sits on top of one of their floats. Rex has beautiful costumes, and throws gifts as well. After Rex, there are many other parades. They continue on until midnight.

Did you know?

Rex created the official colors of Mardi Gras. Purple stands for justice, yellow for power, and green for faith. Rex also gave Mardi Gras its theme song, "If Ever I Cease to Love." The words of the song are really strange:

If ever I cease to love,
May cows lay eggs and fish grow legs.

They say the song was chosen in honor of the Grand Duke Alexei of Russia. While travelling to New York, the Russian prince heard the actress Lydia Thompson sing "If Ever I Cease to Love" and fell in love with her. Lovesick, he followed her shows all the way to New Orleans. Now musicians play the tune during Mardi Gras.

The Krewe of Rex has the biggest parade during Mardi Gras in New Orleans.

What Sets it Apart

What makes Mardi Gras unique are the fans and krewes that come to celebrate each year. Krewe members work hard to entertain the audience. They spend many months making beautiful floats and raising money to pay for all the decorations and gifts. The audience is also dressed in costumes that are as amazing as the ones in the parade. They bring their own art and style to the event. Mardi Gras is a worldwide event that is celebrated in places like France, Germany, Italy, England, the United States, Canada, Mexico, Brazil, and the Caribbean.

The largest Mardi Gras party is in Brazil. In 2011, almost 5 million people celebrated in the city of Rio de Janeiro. Rio is famous for its street parades. From morning until night, people wear daring costumes and dance to samba music. Samba music is played with drums. People sing and dance to the beat.

Carnival dancers in Havana, Cuba

The Samba parade during Carnaval in Brazil

Did you know?

Mardi Gras has different names around the world. In Italy, it is called Carnevale. In England, it is called Pancake Tuesday. And in Mexico and Brazil, it is Carnaval.

Highlights

MASKS AND MASQUERADE BALLS

Masks are everywhere during Mardi Gras. They are usually decorated with glitter, sequins, feathers, and beads. Some only cover the eyes, while others cover the whole face. There are masks you tie onto your face and some you hold up to your face with a stick. Masks are very exciting. You can choose to be another person for the day—like an animal, actor, or clown. You can also get a scary mask and scare all your friends.

Masquerade balls also take place during Mardi Gras. They are big dances where everyone dresses in their fanciest clothes and wears a mask. Many krewes have their own balls. They are usually for members only, but don't feel left out. Many schools have Mardi Gras dances, or you can have your own party at home and tell all your friends to bring cool masks.

Here's a tip:

If you're far away from New Orleans or don't have any big parades near where you live, you can always bring the fun to you. You can have a party at home and dress up in funny costumes with your friends. You can also make your own masks. Just cut out a piece of construction paper in the shape of a mask. Then, decorate it with anything you want. When you're done, glue a popsicle stick to the mask and hold it up to your face. If you need help, ask a parent.

KREWES

Rex and Zulu aren't the only clubs that celebrate Mardi Gras. There are others outside of New Orleans. In Mobile, Alabama, there is a krewe called The Mystics of Time. They have a parade all about dragons. Members of the club ride in floats shaped like dragons and throw gifts from the top. Some dragons are more than a hundred feet long!

In Galveston, Texas, there's the Krewe of Barkus and Meoux. This one is all about pets. There are dogs, cats, guinea pigs, ponies, and more. The animals are also dressed up in costumes. The Krewe of the Munchkins is also from Texas. This one is for children. They ride in floats just like the adults and throw candy and toys to other children.

DID YOU KNOW?

The throws also relate to the theme of the parade. Here are a few krewes with their parade themes and special throws. These examples are from 2014:

Krewe of Excalibur: Their theme was "A Knight at the Renaissance Faire." The krewe threw doubloons and shields.

Krewe of Caesar: The theme was "Game Time." The krewe threw doubloons, plushies shaped like Roman battle axes, and necklaces.

Krewe of Iris: Iris is the oldest all-women Carnival club. Their theme was "Iris Rocks!" The women threw sunglasses, doubloons, and plushies shaped like King Cakes!

THROWS

Throws are the gifts that krewe members throw from the floats. They are usually easy things to catch like T-shirts, Frisbees, beaded necklaces, stuffed animals, plastic cups, small toys, candy, and cake wrapped in clear packages.

Sometimes, the krewes throw doubloons. These are special coins that are collector's items. They have the krewe's name and logo stamped on one side. The other side has the date and year's parade theme. Each krewe has a different parade theme. In the past, there were fun themes like "Dancing in the Streets," "Game Time," "King Arthur Has the Blues" (a parade theme about King Arthur, blues music, and the color blue), and "Louisiana Legends and Landmarks."

HURRICANE KATRINA

On August 29, 2005, New Orleans faced a deadly hurricane. The storm's winds tore through houses and made the waters rise and flood the city. About 80 percent of New Orleans was flooded. Hundreds of people died while thousands ran for shelter or were trapped on the roofs of their homes.

When the waters left the city, people returned to New Orleans, but many did not have homes to go back to. Still, they stayed strong and worked hard to rebuild New Orleans. Surprisingly, New Orleans still had their Mardi Gras in 2006—just six months after Hurricane Katrina. Floats were pulled from the water and there was a lot of reorganizing to do. New Orleans citizens lost many things during the hurricane, but they still did not lose their hope or desire to celebrate.

Around the World

Other parts of Louisiana
Outside of New Orleans, there are other traditions. One is Mardi Gras Courir or Fat Tuesday Run. People wear costumes and ride horses to their neighbors' houses. Then they knock on their doors and ask for food. In return, the riders sing and dance. Afterwards, they use the food to make gumbo.

Mobile, Alabama
In Mobile, people celebrate Mardi Gras with decorated floats, cheerleaders, school marching bands, dancers, and music. Everyone enjoys the parade and looks forward to catching beads, stuffed animals, and toys. Mobile is famous for its moonpie throws. Moonpies are chocolate cakes with white cream fillings.

Rio de Janeiro, Brazil
In Rio, Mardi Gras is known as Carnaval and is celebrated with samba music and dance. The top samba schools make floats with their own special themes, music, and dance styles. Then they compete in the big Samba parade called the Sambadrome. The best float wins a grand prize.

Martinique, Caribbean Islands
In Martinique, people dress up like skeletons, wear feathered hats, and grass skirts. The main part of Carnival is King Carnival. King Carnival is a large statue of a man made from paper. He often pops up during parades. On the last day, people burn him and dance around the flames.

Mardi Gras

The People

Over a million people visit Mardi Gras in New Orleans each year. It gets very crowded, so people hurry to get as close to the parade lines as possible. The closer you are to the lines, the closer you are to seeing the floats and catching some throws. It is a good idea for everyone to arrive early.

Sometimes people bring picnic baskets and chairs. The parades go on and on, so resting and bringing snacks is smart. Some parents bring special ladders with benches on the top so that their children can sit and have a good view of all the sights and throws.

People are also excited to see the famous people that show up during the parade. Sometimes, krewes make celebrities King and Queen of their floats. Throughout the years, jazz legend Louis Armstrong, Britney Spears, Stevie Wonder, Laurence Fishburne, Whoopi Goldberg, Sandra Bullock, Will Ferrell, and Elijah Wood have taken part in the Mardi Gras parade.

A child wears a colorful mask and costume for the Children's Carnival in Port of Spain, Trinidad.

Two young dancers wear face paint and beads at the Caribbean Carnival parade in Rotterdam.

Mardi Gras

Impact

New Orleans is the most popular destination for people wanting to celebrate Mardi Gras in the United States. Visitors are important to the city because they bring business to restaurants, hotels, and stores. This was especially important after Hurricane Katrina, because the money was needed to fix damaged streets and buildings. The city earns about one billion dollars a year from visitors.

Because Mardi Gras gets crowded, it is important for people to book hotels ahead of time. Many hotels have the Mardi Gras spirit before you even step outside. Some have kids' carnivals and parties right inside their doors. Good places to visit are the Louisiana Children's Museum and the Zulu and Rex parades. If it gets too crowded, the museum has an indoor parade you can go to instead. They also offer classes where you can make your own mask!

Above all, Mardi Gras is a unique and unforgettable experience. People dress in their best or funniest outfits, laughter is everywhere, and people give each other presents. Sometimes people who catch gifts turn around and give them to people that didn't get a chance to catch anything. It is a wonderful tradition of kindness and fun.

Laissez les bons temps rouler!
(leh-zay lay bon tom roo-lay)

Let the good times roll!

Glossary

Ash Wednesday: the first day of Lent, a day of fasting

Creole: a French person born in Louisiana, or a person with African American and French blood

doubloons: special coins that krewes throw during parades

fasting: not eating for a period of time or giving up certain foods

float: a decorated stage on wheels that is used to show art, costumes, or people

gumbo: a vegetable stew made with meat and seafood

hurricane: a violent storm with heavy winds and rains

krewe: a private social club that makes parades during Mardi Gras

Lent: a Christian holiday of fasting, prayer, and preparation for Easter

masquerade ball: a dance where everyone wears fancy costumes and masks

medieval: the time of the Middle Ages (500 to 1500 C.E.)

prejudiced: to think badly of someone or something for unfair reasons

slavery: forcing someone to work under harsh conditions for no pay; complete ownership of a person

tradition: a set of beliefs and practices that are passed down from generation to generation